What Will I Do Without You?

For Cass, the very best of friends—S.G.

For Bertie, William, and Maksymilian—P.D.

ISBN 0-439-21718-0

12 11 10 9 8 7 6 5 4 3 2 1   0 1 2 3 4 5/0

Printed in the U.S.A.   09

First Scholastic printing, November 2000

What Will I Do Without You?

Sally Grindley
Illustrated by Penny Dann

SCHOLASTIC INC.
New York Toronto London Auckland Sydney
Mexico City New Delhi Hong Kong

Winter was on its way. Jefferson Bear was fat and his fur wobbled more than ever.

"Shall we go for our walk?" asked Figgy Twosocks.

"No time to walk, Figgy," said Jefferson Bear.
"I need to eat. I'm getting ready to hibernate."
"What's hibernate?" asked Figgy.
"Hibernate is what big brown bears
do in the winter," said Jefferson Bear.
"It's when I go to sleep and
don't wake up until spring."

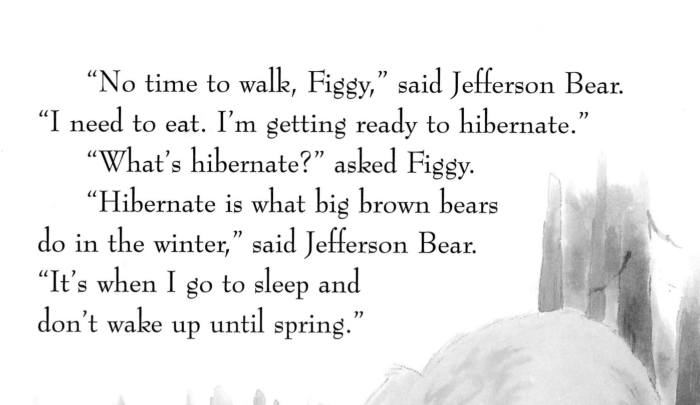

"But what will I do without you?" asked Figgy.

"I'll be back before you know it," said Jefferson Bear.

"I don't want you to go," sulked Figgy Twosocks.

The air turned frosty.
   "Time for bed," yawned Jefferson Bear.
   "Don't go yet," said Figgy Twosocks.
   "I'm sorry little friend—
a big brown bear needs his sleep."

Jefferson Bear hugged her tightly and
disappeared into his cave.
"I'll miss you, JB," called Figgy.

The next morning, it was snowing. Figgy had never seen snow before. She ran to tell Jefferson Bear.

"JB, are you asleep yet?" she called.
A rumbly snore echoed from deep
inside his cave.

Figgy kicked at the snow.
"What good is snow when your
best friend isn't there to share it?"

BIFF! BIFF! BIFF!

Figgy's brothers were
having a snowball fight.

"Can I play?" Figgy Twosocks asked.
"If you want," said Big Smudge

"Take this!" said Floppylugs.

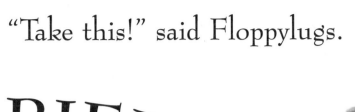

BIFF!

"Stop it!" Figgy squealed. "That hurts."
"You wanted to play" they said,
and ran off laughing.
"You wouldn't do that if JB
were here," she cried.

Then Figgy Twosocks
had an idea . . . .

All day long she pushed and patted the snow.

All day long she rolled and scooped and shaped it.

Finally, she found
three black stones and
a little twig.

She stood back.

"Every time I look at my
Big White Snow Bear, I will
think of JB," she said.

Pow! Pow! Figgy Twosocks woke the
next morning to find Big Smudge and
Floppylugs pelting the Snow Bear.
"Stop it!" she cried. "Leave him alone."
"Crybaby, crybaby," called her
brothers, skipping away.

Figgy Twosocks felt very lonely.
She sobbed a great big sob.

Then she began to feel cross.
If JB was her friend, how could
he leave her for so long?
    PIFF!—she threw a snowball
at the Snow Bear.
    PIFF!—and another.
And another—PIFF!

"Hey, don't do that. You'll ruin it," called a voice.

It was Hoptail the squirrel.

"JB's not my friend anymore,"
said Figgy Twosocks.

"Why not?" asked Hoptail.

"He's not here when I
need him."

"But he needs his sleep,"
said Hoptail. "And I need some
help. I have to find the nuts
I buried in the fall."

Hoptail pointed to places where she thought her food was hidden.

Figgy Twosocks dug down through the snow. "One for you!" she squealed, each time she dug up a nut.

"One for me!" she squealed, each time she dug up a worm.

Day after day, more snow fell. Figgy Twosocks and Hoptail ran through the woods making patterns with their pawprints.

They broke off icicles and watched them melt through their paws.

And together they rebuilt the Big White Snow Bear.

At the end of each day, Figgy Twosocks
went to see the Big White Snow Bear.
  "I hope JB won't mind my having
another friend," she said.

Little by little, the days grew warmer.

"The Snow Bear is melting!" cried Figgy.

"What's happening?"

"Spring is coming," said Hoptail.

Suddenly, Big Smudge and Floppylugs appeared.

They clambered
onto the Snow Bear
and pushed—
HEAVE . . .

WHOOSH!

The head of the Snow Bear
rolled down the hill.

"OUCH! That hurt," growled a great big voice.

Big Smudge and Floppylugs ran away.

There was Jefferson Bear, rubbing his nose.
"That's a fine welcome back," he said.

"JB!" squealed Figgy. "Oh, I've missed you so much. I built a Snow Bear to remind me of you and I hope you don't mind, I've—"

"Yes?" said Jefferson Bear. "I've made a new friend— this is Hoptail."

Jefferson Bear laughed. "Slow down, Figgy. Let's all go for a walk and you can tell me just what you did without me."